TRANSLATING MUSIC

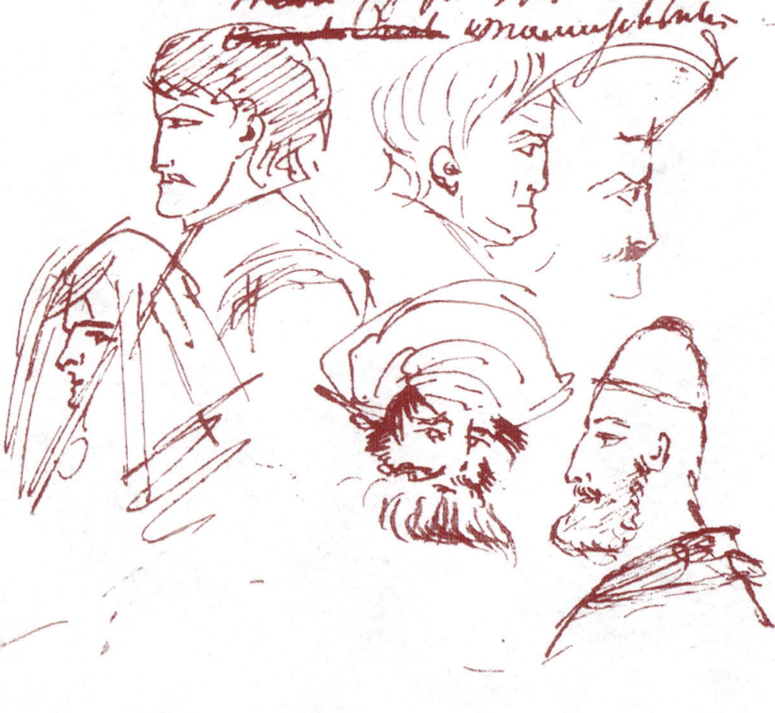

Translating Music

RICHARD PEVEAR

CENTER FOR WRITERS & TRANSLATORS
THE ARTS ARENA

SYLPH EDITIONS

CONTENTS

Preface

THE TWO PIECES BROUGHT TOGETHER here may suggest some-
thing of a translator's itinerary, or at least of one translator's
itinerary, over a quarter century. That and their Russian source
is about all they have in common.

The first, an English version of a tale in verse by Alexander
Pushkin, dates to 1984, though I have made a number of revisions
for this publication. Pushkin is Russia's greatest poet, and his tales
in verse are among his finest works. D. S. Mirsky, in his *History
of Russian Literature,* ventures to say that another of the tales, *Tsar
Saltan,* is "the masterpiece of Russian poetry." "The Tale of the
Preacher and His Man Bumpkin" is a slighter and more playful
piece, imitative of the irregular meters and polysyllabic rhymes
of much Russian popular poetry. It was written in 1830, during
the remarkable autumn that Pushkin spent on his family estate
at Boldino, where he was detained for three months because of a
quarantine. During this most fertile period of his creative life, he
completed his great novel in verse, *Evgeny Onegin,* wrote the five
prose "Tales of Belkin," the four "little tragedies" ("The Covetous
Knight," "Mozart and Salieri," "The Stone Guest," and "The Feast
During the Plague"), a long poem in octaves entitled "The Little
House in Kolomna," another tale in verse, "The Tale of the She-
Bear," and some of his most beautiful lyric poems.

"To translate poetry is impossible," Voltaire wisely said,
adding: "Can one translate music?" He was right, of course.
Yet poets, who should know that better than anyone else, have
always been tempted to try the impossible, and in English poetry
alone the list of major poet-translators begins with Chaucer and
continues to the present day. The poet that I was in 1984 had
already yielded to the temptation more than once.

Since then, with a few lapses, my work as a translator has been confined to prose, and mainly, in collaboration with Larissa Volokhonsky, to Russian prose of the ninteenth century. As a result of which, in August 2006, we were invited to an international conference on translating Tolstoy, held at Yasnaya Polyana, Tolstoy's estate in Tula province, some 120 kilometers south of Moscow. The second piece included here, "The Translator's Inner Voice," is a revised and expanded version of my contribution to the conference. As we were then at work on a translation of *War and Peace,* my thoughts and examples refer to that book (which Tolstoy refused to call a novel). The principles of translation I tried to define there are very different from the principles of translating poetry, the difficulties of which (paradoxically) require considerably more freedom from the translator. But, as I hope to have shown, in both cases it is a question of translating music.

Richard Pevear
Paris, 2007

Сказка о попе и о работнике его Балде

The Tale of the Preacher and His Man Bumpkin

Alexander Pushkin

Жил-был поп,
Толоконный лоб.
Пошёл поп по базару
Посмотреть кой-какого товару.
Навстречу ему Балда
Идёт, сам не зная куда.
«Что, батька, так рано поднялся?
Чего ты взыскался?»
Поп ему в ответ: «Нужен мне работник:
Повар, конюх и плотник.
А где найти мне такого
Служителя не слишком дорогого?»
Балда говорит: «Буду служить тебе славно,
Усердно и очень исправно,
В год за три щелка тебе по лбу.
Есть же мне давай варёную полбу».
Призадумался поп,
Стал себе почёсывать лоб.
Щёлк щелку ведь розь.
Да понадеялся он на русский авось.
Поп говорит Балде: «Ладно.
Не будет нам обоим накладно.
Поживи-ка на моём подворье,
Окажи своё усердие и проворье».
Живёт Балда в поповом доме,
Спит себе на соломе,
Ест за четверых,
Работает за семерых;
Досветла всё у него пляшет,
Лошадь запряжёт, полосу вспашет.
Печь затопит, всё заготовит, закупит,
Яичко испечёт да сам и облупит.
Попадья Балдой не нахвалится,
Поповна о Балде лишь и печалится,
Попёнок зовёт его тятей;
Кашу заварит, нянчится с дитятей.
Только поп один Балду не любит,
Никогда его не приголубит,
О расплате думает частенько;

There once was a preacher,
A mush-headed creature.
He stood in the marketplace one day
Looking over the goods on display.
Just then Bumpkin was passing by,
Going who knows where and who knows why,
And as he passed he tipped his hat:
"You're up early, preacher, why is that?"
"I want a man," the preacher said,
"To tar the roof and mend the shed,
Milk the cow and clean the stable,
Cook the meals and set the table,
Dot every jot and cross every title,
And I want to pay him very little.
Can I find such an honest man?" he sighed.
"You just did," Bumpkin replied.
"In return for three flicks on your brow,
To be delivered a year from now,
I'll do your work with skill and zeal.
Is it a deal?
I'll also want some porridge."
The preacher scratched his forehead.
There are flicks and flicks, he thought.
But, after all, why not?
"A deal," he said, taking Bumpkin's arm.
"Come and live on my farm.
Show us your zeal and skill,
And you can eat your fill.
Neither of us will be worse off!"
So Bumpkin slept in the loft,
Ate like four men and worked like seven.
The morning star still shone in heaven
When things were already at the boil.
He hitched the horses, plowed the soil,
Lit the stove and stocked the shelf,
Cooked an egg and peeled it himself.
The preacher's wife overflowed with praise.
The daughter wandered in a daze
Thinking only of him. The little boy

Время идёт, и срок уж близенько.
Поп ни ест, ни пьёт, ночи не спит:
Лоб у него заране трещит.
Вот он попадье признаётся:
«Так и так: что делать остаётся?»
Ум у бабы догадлив,
На всякие хитрости повадлив.
Попадья говорит: «Знаю средство,
Как удалить от нас такое бедство:
Закажи Балде службу, чтоб стало ему невмочь,
А требуй, чтоб он её исполнил точь-в-точь.
Тем ты и лоб от расправы избавишь
И Балду-то без расплаты отправишь».
Стало на сердце попа веселее.
Начал он глядеть на Балду посмелее.
Вот он кричит: «Поди-ка сюда,
Верный мой работник Балда.
Слушай: платить обязались черти
Мне оброк по самой моей смерти;
Лучшего б не надобно дохода,
Да есть на них недоимки за три года.
Как наешься ты своей полбы,
Собери-ка с чертей оброк мне полный».
Балда, с попом понапрасну не споря,
Пошёл, сел у берега моря;
Там он стал верёвку крутить
Да конец её в море мочить.
Вот из моря вылез старый Бес:
«Зачем ты, Балда, к нам залез?» –
«Да вот верёвкой хочу море морщить
Да вас, проклятое племя, корчить».
Беса старого взяла тут унылость.
«Скажи, за что такая немилость?» –
«Как за что? Вы не платите оброка,
Не помните положенного срока;
Вот ужо будет нам потеха,
Вам, собакам, великая помеха».–
«Балдушка, погоди ты морщить море,
Оброк сполна ты получишь вскоре.

Began to call him "Daddy." Joy
Was shared by all except the preacher,
Who had a suspicious nature.
Glancing at Bumpkin on the sly,
He could think only of the day
When he must pay the reckoning.
Time passed, fate was beckoning.
He could not sleep or stand or sit.
His forehead was about to split
With apprehension. "Thus and so,"
He told his wife, "what shall I do?"
A woman's wits are quick
And keen on every sort of trick.
"I'll tell you how to stay the master
And save us from disaster.
Give Bumpkin an impossible task,
And make him do just what you ask.
He fails, you send him packing,
And spare your head a smacking."
The preacher cheered up. He began
To look more boldly at his man.
"Bumpkin, come here, you clever fellow!
I have a job for you!" he bellowed.
"Listen. By an old arrangement,
There are certain devils who pay me rent –
A nice sum, I've lived on it for years.
But now they've fallen in arrears.
As soon as you've had your porridge, go
Collect all that they owe."
Bumpkin made no argument.
He ate his porridge and then went
Straight to the shore of the sea, sat down,
And twirled a long rope round and round,
Churning the sea to the very bottom.
An old devil crawled out and besought him:
"What have you, Bumpkin, to do with us?"
"Oh, I just wanted to cause a fuss
And make your cursed tribe jump a little."
A single tear began to trickle

Погоди, вышлю к тебе внука».
Балда мыслит: «Этого провести не штука!»
Вынырнул подосланный бесёнок,
Замяукал он, как голодный котёнок:
«Здравствуй, Балда мужичок;
Какой тебе надобен оброк?
Об оброке век мы не слыхали,
Не было чертям такой печали.
Ну, так и быть – возьми, да с уговору,
С общего нашего приговору –
Чтобы впредь не было никому горя:
Кто скорее из нас обежит около моря,
Тот и бери себе полный оброк,
Между тем там приготовят мешок».
Засмеялся Балда лукаво:
«Что ты это выдумал, право?
Где тебе тягаться со мною,
Со мною, с самим Балдою?
Экого послали супостата!
Подожди-ка моего меньшого брата».
Пошёл Балда в ближний лесок,
Поймал двух зайков, да в мешок.
К морю опять он приходит,
У моря бесёнка находит.

Балда   Бѣсёнокъ

Down the old devil's wrinkled face.
"Tell me, why are we in disgrace?"
"Why? You know you agreed to pay
A certain sum on a certain day,
And yet you haven't paid for years.
Wait and see, it won't be tears
You shed soon, but your patchy skins!
What fun we'll have!" "Now, Bumpikins,
There's no need to resort to threats.
Of course we'll settle our debts.
I'll send my grandson to discuss the matter.
And do stop churning up the water!"
The grandson shouldn't be much trouble,
Bumpkin thought. The water bubbled,
A little devil came creeping out
And, like a hungry kitten, meowed:
"Greetings, Mister Bumpkin, sir.
As for the rent to which you refer,
This is the first we've heard about it.
That's not to say you'll go without it.
But to avoid unpleasantness
In future, allow me to suggest
A little race around the sea.
Whoever wins will take the fee.
They'll put up the money down below.
Well, shall we have a go?"
"Against me, Bumpkin, you want to run?
They must have sent their silliest one!
Wait, I'll fetch my little brother."
He went to the woods and without much bother
Caught two hares, stuffed them in a sack,
And in a trice came back
To the devil waiting on the shore.
He held one hare up by the ear:
"Now dance to my music, little one."
Then turned to the devil: "You're too young
To vie with me. It's a waste of time.
Try beating this little brother of mine.
One, two, three – catch as catch can!"

Держит Балда за уши одного зайку:
«Попляши-тка ты под нашу балалайку;
Ты, бесёнок, ещё молоденек,
Со мною тягаться слабенек;
Это было б лишь времени трата.
Обгони-ка сперва моего брата.
Раз, два, три! догоняй-ка».
Пустились бесёнок и зайка:
Бесёнок по берегу морскому,
А зайка в лесок до дому.
Вот, море кругом обежавши,
Высунув язык, мордку поднявши,
Прибежал бесёнок, задыхаясь,
Весь мокрёшенек, лапкой утираясь,
Мысля: дело с Балдою сладит.
Глядь-а Балда братца гладит,
Приговаривая: «Братец мой любимый,
Устал, бедняжка! отдохни, родимый».
Бесёнок оторопел,
Хвостик поджал, совсем присмирел,
На братца поглядывает боком.
«Погоди, – говорит, – схожу за оброком».
Пошёл к деду, говорит: «Беда!
Обогнал меня меньшой Балда!»
Старый Бес стал тут думать думу.
А Балда наделал такого шуму,
Что всё море смутилось
И волнами так и расходилось.
Вылез бесёнок: «Полно, мужичок,
Вышлем тебе весь оброк –
Только слушай. Видишь ты палку эту?
Выбери себе любую мету.
Кто далее палку бросит,
Тот пускай и оброк уносит.
Что ж? боишься вывихнуть ручки?
Чего ты ждешь?» – «Да жду вон этой тучки;
Зашвырну туда твою палку,
Да и начну с вами, чертями, свалку».
Испугался бесёнок да к деду,

The devil and the hare both ran.
The devil raced along the shore;
Home to the woods dashed the little hare.
Gasping for breath, tongue hanging out,
Sweat dripping off his hairy snout,
In no time the devil finished the race.
He wiped his paw across his face,
Sure that he'd settled Bumpkin's affair.
Bumpkin sat stroking a little hare,
Saying, "Brother dear, our race is won.
Rest now, rest, my little one."
The young devil was flabbergasted.
Tail between his legs, exhausted,
He looked askance at Bumpkin's bunny.
"Wait," he said, "I'll fetch the money."
He went to his grandpa: "Catastrophe!
Bumpkin's brother has beaten me!"
The old devil began to pout.
Bumpkin twirled his rope about,
Thrashing the sea from bottom to top.
The young devil crawled out, crying: "Stop!
We agree to pay you all we owe –
On one condition. If you can throw
This stick higher than I can, then
You get the money. But if I win,
You leave us in peace and go without.
Well, what are you waiting for?" "That cloud…
I'll throw your stick as high as that.
Then you and I will have a chat."
The devil got scared. Away he ran
To report that Bumpkin had won again.
Bumpkin's rope made the waters roar,
Tormenting the devils more and more.
At last the small devil scrambled out.
"What on earth is all this rout?
You'll get your money. All you have to do…"
"No, this time it will be me, not you,
Who decides what the conditions will be,"
Said Bumpkin. "You'll get a task from me

Рассказывать про Балдову победу,
А Балда над морем опять шумит
Да чертям верёвкой грозит.
Вылез опять бесёнок: «Что ты хлопочешь?
Будет тебе оброк, коли захочешь…» –
«Нет, – говорит Балда, –
Теперь моя череда,
Условия сам назначу,
Задам тебе, вражонок, задачу.
Посмотрим, какова у тебя сила.
Видишь, там сивая кобыла?
Кобылу подыми-тка ты
Да неси её полверсты;
Снесёшь кобылу, оброк уж твой;
Не снесёшь кобылы, ан будет он мой».
Бедненький бес
Под кобылу подлез,
Понатужился,
Понапружился,
Приподнял кобылу, два шага шагнул,
На третьем упал, ножки протянул.
А Балда ему: «Глупый ты бес,

попъ талаконный лобъ,

That will prove how strong you really are.
Do you see that gray mare over there?
Lift her and carry her half a mile,
And keep your money with a smile.
But if you can't, the money's mine."
The little devil crept up behind
The great gray mare, slipped underneath,
Drew a deep breath,
Strained and struggled,
Raised her a little,
Took one step, two steps, and at the third
Went sprawling in the dirt.
"Foolish devil!" Bumpkin laughed.
"You're no match for me by half!
Your arms couldn't hold her up, but watch –
My legs and I will win the match."
Bumpkin jumped up on the mare
And rode a half mile down the shore,
Kicking up a cloud of dust.
Frightened, the little devil rushed
To bring his grandpapa the news.
Since there was nothing else to do,
The devils put money in a sack
And heaved it onto Bumpkin's back.
He went off, groaning under the weight.
The preacher was standing at the gate
And saw him coming. In fear of his life,
He ran and hid behind his wife.
Bumpkin found him cowering there,
Threw down the sack, and demanded his share.
The poor preacher offered up his head.
One flick and he flew over the shed.
Flick, and he couldn't speak or hear.
Flick, and he lost his wits for a year.
And all the while Bumpkin kept repeating:
"The cheaper the goods, the worse the beating."

Куда ж ты за нами полез?
И руками-то снести не смог,
А я, смотри, снесу промеж ног».
Сел Балда на кобылку верхом
Да версту проскакал, так что пыль столбом.
Испугался бесёнок и к деду
Пошёл рассказывать про такую победу.
Делать нечего – черти собрали оброк
Да на Балду взвалили мешок.
Идёт Балда, покрякивает,
А поп, завидя Балду, вскакивает,
За попадью прячется,
Со страху корячится.
Балда его тут отыскал,
Отдал оброк, платы требовать стал.
Бедный поп
Подставил лоб:
С первого щелка
Прыгнул поп до потолка;
Со второго щелка
Лишился поп языка;
А с третьего щелка
Вышибло ум у старика.
А Балда приговаривал с укоризной:
«Не гонялся бы ты, поп, за дешевизной».

The Translator's Inner Voice

A Talk

I would like to begin these few remarks with a tribute to our predecessor, Boris de Schloezer, one of the best translators of Russian literature into French – also a distinguished writer, critic, and musicologist – who was born in Vitebsk in 1881 and died in Paris in 1969. In the preface to his translation of *War and Peace* he speaks with an intelligence born of experience about the problems of translating Tolstoy. Having shared his experience, I hope to borrow some of that intelligence from him here.

When I mentioned to a Russian friend that we were translating *War and Peace,* he said, "Well, that's easier than Dostoevsky. Tolstoy wrote good Russian prose." In de Schloezer's preface, on the other hand, we find a rather surprising assertion, one that perhaps only a translator would be likely to make:

> *Il faut avouer avec tout le respect dû à celui que Tourguéniev appelait « le grand écrivain de la terre russe », que musicale, la langue de* Guerre et Paix *ne l'est nullement, que* Guerre et Paix *est même très mal écrit.*

> It must be admitted with all due respect to him whom Turgenev called "the great writer of the Russian land," that the language of *War and Peace* is not at all musical, that *War and Peace* is even very badly written.

He goes on to say that, especially in *War and Peace,* Tolstoy makes crude errors that are not justified by anything and that not even a schoolboy would make; that there is in the very language of *War and Peace* a carelessness that one does not find elsewhere in Tolstoy's work, and which is all the more surprising in that the text was recopied several times and much corrected in proofs.

The questions that de Schloezer raises implicitly here are those that I want to raise explicitly: what do we mean by good and bad writing; more precisely, what is "artistic prose" and how should it be translated?

Early in his preface, de Schloezer states the general problem of translation clearly:

> What is a good translation? One, they say, that while remaining faithful to the original, uses a correct French, which "does not feel like a translation," according to the current expression, thus giving the reader the impression that he is reading a text written directly in his mother tongue. The transposition is then perfect: the author's thought is preserved while being wedded to a new form. *But how can it have been preserved?* Doesn't being faithful to an author mean preserving the structure, the tone, the pace of his language as much as its explicit meaning? *War and Peace* or *The Brothers Karamazov* could not be written in French any more than *Madame Bovary* or *Le Rouge et le Noir* could be written in Russian, and that for a thousand reasons, of which the first, which is amply sufficient, is that the language of a novel, of a story, no less than of a poem, is not the clothing of a certain mode of thinking, of perceiving, of feeling, of loving, but is that mode itself. Here the habit makes the monk.

The contradiction seems insoluble. Translation, if not a lost cause, is, as de Schloezer says, "a strange, paradoxical operation...Yet we do translate, and good translations do exist, even excellent ones. They are precisely those which bring the paradox fully to light, which push it to the point of scandal." I want to consider what he may have meant by that.

Discussions of translation generally turn around the notions of faithfulness and freedom. But faithfulness to what? Freedom from what, and for what? Whom does the translator listen to? What inner voice guides him in this paradoxical operation? Publishers now have at their disposal a computer program which assesses what they call the "readability level" of a text – say, of a novel or a translation of a novel that is submitted to them. A certain quantity of polysyllabic words or complex sentences lowers the readability level. For marketing purposes, a high readability level is considered good. Books with a high readability level are known as "reader friendly." When we were translating *Anna Karenina*, we were told by our editors that what they wanted was a "reader-friendly" translation, and that the version we had submitted was far from "reader friendly." I told them that if there was anything Tolstoy was *not* it was reader friendly. Fortunately, we were able to have the translation our way, but I wonder how a younger or less experienced translator would have fared.

There are other editorial computer programs that detect such supposed faults of style as repetitions, sentence fragments, syntactic inversions, and even "new obscenities." So that when Tolstoy has Kitty Scherbatsky exclaim, "I do love balls!" or when Anna asks Vronsky, "Did you come recently?" all the lights start flashing. I suspect that the increasing uniformity and lack of style in contemporary writing may have something to do with the application of these programs – whether by publishers or by the writers themselves, since they are "internalized," as Americans like to say, in most word processors.

But even if the program is internalized, it is hardly an "inner voice." It is rather a mechanical interference in the "strange, paradoxical operation" of translation. There is another sort of voice that is truly internal and much more insidious. It is the voice inside the translator that says, "How do we usually say that in English?" or, even worse, "You can't say that in English." It is this voice that says, "A translation should not feel like a translation," a translation should read "smoothly," it should be "idiomatic." The word "idiomatic" elicits immediate and universal consent. But what good writer ever wrote in smooth, natural, idiomatic language? In transforming everyday language into an artistic medium, a writer marks it in a specific way, and makes use of a far wider range of possibilities, of sounds, of tone colors, of rhythms, of vocabulary and syntax, than are used in normal "idiomatic" communication. Andrei Sinyavsky, in his book *In Gogol's Shadow*, goes so far as to define artistic prose as "the impossibility of saying anything in a simple and direct way." Those who insist that a translation be "idiomatic" do not seem to realize that they are imposing their own, often very narrow, limits on the original. Who determines the standard of the "idiomatic," and why should it be applied to something so idiolectic as a great work of literature? Yet it is applied, not only by editors or reviewers, but by translators themselves.

The results of the idiomatic approach are well illustrated in Anthony Briggs's translation of *War and Peace*, published by Penguin in 2005. Mr. Briggs states his principles in an afterword:

> Without ever drifting too far away from the original, it does seem reasonable to aim for the kind of English that would have occurred naturally in its context and now sounds appropriate.
>
> Another way to look at this is to imagine how the average Russian reads *War and Peace* and to try to recapture something similar in the translated text. Tolstoy's literary style has its faults...but by and large he is an easy read for a Russian (and comparatively easy to translate). Stylistic angularities, shocks and surprises are infrequent, and the dialogue in particular is individualized but always natural. It seems most important to ensure in any translation the same kind of smooth reading and varied but realistic-sounding dialogue.

I don't know what a translator would gain by imagining "how the average Russian reads *War and Peace*" and trying to "recapture something similar in the translated text." It would almost certainly take him rather far from the original. But let me give some examples of what Mr. Briggs's method leads to in practice.

> Oh! He's got his head screwed on has old Kutuzov. What a character!

The phrasing may indeed be idiomatic, but where does the idiom come from? The speaker in this case is Prince Vassily Kuragin, a haughty and rather frivolous Russian aristocrat, and a person of mincing delicacy. What Tolstoy actually has him say is:

> Oh, he's a most intelligent man, Prince Kutuzov, *et quel caractère!*

Or take the moment when M. de Beausset, a former courtier of the Bourbons who has become prefect of the imperial palace,

unveils a portrait of Napoleon's son before the emperor.
Mr. Briggs translates:

> De Beausset, practised courtier that he was, performed a
> nifty backward two-step, half-twisting but not once turning
> his back, and in one movement whipped off the cover...

Again there is a strange sort of verbal pollution from some
extraneous source (that leaky vessel christened "the idiomatic").
Tolstoy allows the old man considerably more dignity and grace:

> Beausset, with courtly adroitness, not showing his back,
> half turned and withdrew two steps, at the same time
> snatching off the cover...

Here are some further examples of what Mr. Briggs calls "the
kind of English that would have occurred naturally in its context
and now sounds appropriate" and that in fact is a patchwork of
ready-made phrases completely foreign to Tolstoy.

> It was whispered that the two Empresses had adopted
> polarized attitudes towards these difficult circumstances.

> From the city's rumour mill she heard about the
> Rostovs' situation...

> These arrangements, obscure and confused as they
> are in this written form – if we can take time off from
> worshipping Napoleon's military genius and look at his
> actual instructions – boil down to four points, four basic
> instructions, none of which was carried out, or ever
> could have been.

> Pierre was greatly affected by the curious idea that of
> all those thousands of men, alive and kicking, young
> and old, who had been staring at his hat with such easy
> amusement, twenty thousand were inexorably destined
> to be wounded or killed, maybe men he had seen with
> his own eyes.
> "...and they think my hat's funny! It's weird!"
> thought Pierre.

> But it wasn't this that made her unrecognizable. No one
> would have recognized her when he entered the room

because when he had first glanced at her the face and eyes that in days gone by had always glowed with a half-suppressed smile of sheer *joie de vivre* had held no trace of a smile. They were anybody's eyes, kindly, brooding, quizzical, and sad.

In his effort to match his *War and Peace* with what he presumes to be his English reader of today, Mr. Briggs has sacrificed the rhythm, the voicing, the character, and at times the meaning of the original. The following are our versions of the same passages, for comparison:

> It was recounted in whispers how differently from each other the two empresses behaved in these difficult circumstances.

> From town rumors she learned about the situation of the Rostovs...

> This disposition, drawn up quite vaguely and confusedly – if one allows oneself to consider Napoleon's instructions without religious awe of his genius – contained four points, four instructions. Not one of them was or could have been carried out.

> The strange notion that among those thousands of men, alive, healthy, young and old, who had stared with merry surprise at his hat, twenty thousand were probably destined for wounds and death (maybe the same ones he had seen), struck Pierre.
> "...yet they get surprised at my hat! Strange!" thought Pierre.

> But that was not what had made her unrecognizable: it had been impossible to recognize her in the first moment, as he came in, because on that face, in the eyes of which formerly there had always shone a secret smile of the joy of life, now, when he had come in and glanced at her for the first time, there had been not even the shadow of a smile; there had been only eyes – attentive, kind, and sadly questioning.

Translation is not the transfer of a detachable "meaning"

from one language to another. It is a dialogue between two languages. It takes place in a space between two languages. And most often also between two historical moments. Much of the real value of translation as an art comes from that unique situation. It is not exclusively the language of arrival or the time of the translator and reader that should be privileged. We all know, in the case of *War and Peace*, that we are reading a nineteenth-century Russian novel; it should not read as if it was written yesterday in English. That fact allows the twenty-first century translator a different range of possibilities than may exist for a twenty-first century writer. It allows for an enrichment of the translator's own language, rather than the imposition of his language on the foreign original. That is what translation was in the Elizabethan age, with the great style- and language-forming translations of Christopher Marlowe, George Chapman, and Arthur Golding. And what a loss it would have been to Shakespeare, and to us, if he had not had Florio's Montaigne and North's Plutarch! So, too, in the twentieth century, the possibilities of English poetry were greatly enlarged by Ezra Pound's translations of the troubadours, of classical Chinese poetry, of the Anglo-Saxon "Seafarer." To move from this fertile middle ground towards either extreme – that is, towards interlinear literalness or total accommodation to the language and time of arrival – is to lose those possibilities that exist only in the space between two times and languages. The philosopher Paul Ricoeur put the matter very well in a talk he gave at UNESCO in Paris, on April 28, 2004, shortly before his death (I quote, and translate, from a revised version published shortly afterwards in the newspaper *Le Monde*):

> Translation is the mediation between the plurality of cultures and the unity of humanity ... the astonishing phenomenon of translation is that it transfers the meaning of one language to another or of one culture to another, not making them identical, however, but offering only an equivalent. Translation is the phenomenon of equivalence without identity. In this it serves the project of humanity, without breaking down the initial plurality. This last is a figure of humanity engendered by translation in the very flesh of plurality.

The translator should listen, then, not to the strictures of editorial software, not to readability analysts, not to advocates of a "smooth, modern rendering" in that "idiomatic English" which is merely the lowest common denominator of current verbal exchange – but to the original. Tolstoy did not write good or bad Russian prose; he wrote Tolstoyan prose; his language is an artistic medium; it is all of a piece. It is indeed the habit that makes the monk. What the translator must seek in his own language is the equivalent of that specific artistic medium. He must have the freedom in his own language to be faithful to the original.

At the conclusion of his preface, de Schloezer comes to what he considers the essence of Tolstoy's prose – its concern, not with formal beauty, not with artistic play, but with speaking the *truth* as perceived by his eye and his conscience. "All the forces of his imagination, his power of evocation and expression, converge on that one single goal. Outside any other religious or moral considerations, Tolstoy when he writes obeys one imperative which is the foundation of what one might call his literary ethic. That imperative is not imposed on the artist by the moralist, it is the voice of the artist himself." De Schloezer speaks of the "crushing mass" of heterogeneous materials that went into the composition of *War and Peace* – the hundreds of characters, the documents, letters, lyrical effusions, minute descriptions, general reflections. But he adds:

> This mass, however, is admirably put together; there are no faults in this immense polyphonic construction whose slow unfolding the reader follows without effort. But the material that Tolstoy treats preserves from its origins a certain roughness, something unpolished, which explains and partly justifies the carelessness of the writing. The stylistic deficiencies I have pointed out are bound up with the conception Tolstoy had of his novel, with what he wanted more or less consciously to express in it and which otherwise he undoubtedly could not have expressed.

That, I think, is the essential point. It is to this artistic unity of the work itself, of the thing made, with all its particularities, even its faults or deficiencies, that the translator must be as faithful as possible.

That task demands a certain discipline of attention, which I will try to illustrate with a few examples. They all come from Volume IV of *War and Peace*, because we happened to be working on Volume IV when we were invited to the colloquium at Yasnaya Polyana and I began looking for interesting examples; but they could easily be multiplied back through the first three volumes.

My first example is a sentence made up of only two words; in fact, made up of one word used first as a noun, then as a verb: *Kápli kápali* ("Drops dripped"). It comes from Volume IV, Part 3, Chapter 10. You may remember the context: it is Petya Rostov's last night, one of the most haunting moments in the book. This is the first sentence of a paragraph made up of four brief, separate, staccato sentences, four extremely ordinary observations in themselves, which acquire a lyrical intensity owing solely to their sound and rhythm: *Kápli kápali. Shyól tíkhii góvor. Lóshadi zarzháli i podrális. Khrapél któ-to* ("Drops dripped. Quiet talk went on. Horses neighed and scuffled. Someone snored"). That is the whole paragraph. Stylistically, nothing could be simpler. *Kápli kápali.* The sentence is striking in Russian, but not odd. It seems to pose no problem for the English translator; it all but translates itself. In both cases, the sound is most of the meaning. However, in the three other English versions I have looked at, I find the following:

> CONSTANCE GARNETT (1904): The branches dripped.
> LOUISE & AYLMER MAUDE (1927): The trees were dripping.
> ANTHONY BRIGGS (2005): Raindrops dripped.

Why is it that none of them translates it as "Drops dripped"? It may be instructive to try to imagine the mental process that led to these different versions. Is it that the translators were frightened by the very simplicity of the original? That they found "Drops dripped" a little ridiculous (isn't it a pleonasm? what else can drops do?). Or that they wanted to avoid the repetition? But should the rule – if it is one – about avoiding repetitions be applied in a case like this, when the repetition is there in the original, is even more marked, and is precisely what the author intended? There may be languages for which the sentence poses more of a problem. I'm told, for instance, that while

French has the noun *goutte* ("drop") and the verb *goutter* ("to drip"), it would be very bad French to say *"Les gouttes gouttaient."* Which is no doubt why de Schloezer says *"Les gouttes tombaient"* ("The drops fell"). English in this case happens to be in luck. Yet for these three translators, some other voice interfered in the process and advised them to shy away from Tolstoy's boldness.

Here is another example of the same sort of stylistic compactness: *Prosnúlas lyubóv, i prosnúlas zhizn.* It is from Volume IV, Part 4, Chapter 3, when Natasha cares for her mother after they learn of Petya's death. It is a question, this time, not of sense impression, but of psychological insight. Again the simplicity, in this case the very deliberate rhetorical matter-of-factness, and all that it implies about Tolstoy's understanding of Natasha's inner life, is clearly intended. And again it seems to pose no problem for the English translator: "Love awoke, and life awoke." When I look at the three other translations, however, I find:

> GARNETT: Love was awakened, and life waked with it.
> MAUDES: Love awoke, and so did life.
> BRIGGS: When love reawakened, life reawakened.

In each of the three, the all-important tone of the original, created by the exact rhetorical balance of the phrasing, is lost, though each loses it in a different way. It seems as if the translators deliberately set out to put something awkward and flat in place of the expressive poise of the original. All that Tolstoy leaves unsaid is implied in that tone: *Prosnúlas lyubóv, i prosnúlas zhízn.* What led the translators to alter the original, when the right translation is so obvious? But can one really speak of a "right" translation? Aren't the other versions equally valid? Don't they convey the same meaning? Am I not being too judgmental? Am I not guilty of abject literalism? I don't think so. What makes our translation "right" is not its literalness but its faithfulness to Tolstoy's voice, to what de Schloezer refers to as "the structure, tone, and pace of his language," that is, to the quality of his perception reflected in his words. To alter the style is to lose much of the meaning as well. That loss is not inevitable; it is not forced upon the translator by the difference of languages. We can just as well say in English what Tolstoy says in Russian. And yet some nagging editorial voice whispered in these translators' ears: "We wouldn't say it that way" or "That's not idiomatic," and they followed that other voice instead of listening to Tolstoy.

My third example is more problematic: *Dyévyat dnei póslye ostavléniya Moskvyí, v Peterburg priyékhal póslannii ot Kutúzova c ofitsiálnym izvéstiem ob ostavlénii Moskvyí.* That is the opening sentence of Volume iv, Part i, Chapter 3. Here I'll admit that I was pulled up short. Translating what is there in the Russian, we arrive at the following: "Nine days after the abandoning of Moscow, a messenger from Kutuzov reached Petersburg with official news of the abandoning of Moscow." Perhaps this time we do indeed have an example of what de Schloezer means when he says that Tolstoy "makes errors that even a schoolboy would not make." Shouldn't the translator give the original a little "brushing up" here? De Schloezer does just that himself. His version reads: *"Neuf jours après la chute de Moscou, un envoyé de Koutouzov apporta à Pétersbourg la nouvelle officielle de l'abandon."* The repetitions are all neatly eliminated. What do my three English translators do? More or less the same thing.

> GARNETT: Nine days after the abandonment of Moscow, a courier from Kutuzov reached Petersburg with the official news of the surrender of Moscow.
> MAUDES: Nine days after the abandonment of Moscow, a messenger from Kutuzov reached Petersburg with the official announcement of that event.
> BRIGGS: Nine days after the abandonment of Moscow a courier from Kutuzov reached Petersburg with an official announcement of the surrender of the city.

Obviously, Tolstoy's repetitions simply would not go down with any of them. But what besides the most stubborn literalism can justify a translator in keeping them? The first book I translated in my life, some 34 years ago, was *Les Dieux*, by the French philosopher Alain. Commenting on a problem in biblical criticism, he says: "Repeated experience has taught me never to change a text before I have tried seriously to understand it." I asked myself seriously: since we all can see the awkward, almost ludicrous repetitiousness of this sentence, why did Tolstoy not see it? Was it simple inadvertence? Nabokov, who was a scrupulous stylist himself, comments on a similar instance in Part One of *Anna Karenina* (see his *Lectures on Russian Literature*). Tolstoy is describing the bustle following an accident in the Moscow railway station: "The stationmaster, in a peaked cap of an extraordinary color, also ran past. Evidently something extraordinary had happened." Nabokov notes: "There is of course no actual connection between the [hat and the event], but the repetition is characteristic of Tolstoy's style with its rejection of false elegancies and its readiness to admit any robust awkwardness if that is the shortest way to sense." But isn't he merely covering up for a teammate? How can such "robust awkwardness" be "the shortest way to sense"? And in any case what is a translator to do with it? Shouldn't he step in and correct the master's infelicity?

Listen to it again: "Nine days after the abandoning of Moscow, a messenger from Kutuzov reached Petersburg with official news of the abandoning of Moscow." The repetition certainly makes felt the inevitable delay between an event and its official announcement, which comes as a sort of belated echo. But it does more than that; it makes the delay felt in a certain way. If we hear it as intentionally ironic (which I think it is), then it points beyond mere verbal irony to a deeper human irony that is thematically central to *War and Peace* – the absolute discrepancy between those who are involved in events and those who hear "official reports" of them; between the battlefield and the capital; between the front line and headquarters – or, to use Tolstoy's terms in part two of the Epilogue, between art and history. The apparent awkwardness of the repetition is justified because it is there in the human situation itself. I am certain that Tolstoy realized it and intended it. To correct it according to some general stylistic principle is to lose the specific artistic point.

My fourth example is the following: *Dyéti na stúlyakh yékhali v Moskvú i priglasíli yeyó s sobóyu.* This is from the Epilogue, Part I, Chapter 9, when Countess Marya, feeling the weight of her husband's displeasure, goes to see her children after dinner. It is a slightly more extended example of the compact expressiveness of Tolstoy's prose, and of why it is important for the translator to let himself be taught by the original. Our translation reads: "The children were riding to Moscow on chairs and invited her to join them." Our three fellow translators felt a need to explain what the children were doing:

GARNETT: The children were sitting on chairs playing at driving to Moscow, and invited her to join them.

MAUDES: The children were playing at "going to Moscow" in a carriage made of chairs, and invited her to go with them.

BRIGGS: The children were perched on chairs playing at driving to Moscow, and they invited her to join them.

The addition of explanatory phrases and comments, where the author only suggests, is one of the worst banes to afflict translators.* I will give another example of it, by way of digression: in Nikolai Gogol's *Dead Souls*, Korobochka's housekeeper comes from the larder carrying honey in a wooden *pobratíma*. Few Russian readers know exactly what a *pobratíma* is. It has been translated into English as a "tub," a "dish," a "stoup," but one well-known translator rendered it as "a round wooden vessel with a narrow neck." That is an extreme case of explanatory translation, but the practice is more common than one might think. Here the whole charm of Tolstoy's sentence comes precisely from the fact that he does not explain in an adult way what the children are doing; he enters into the spirit of their game by the very phrasing he uses to describe it, and the whole atmosphere of the moment is suddenly there, naïve, natural, alive: *Dyéti na stúlyakh yékhali v Moskvú . . .* – "The children were riding to Moscow on chairs . . ." Because children don't "play at" riding; in their imaginations they *are* riding.

My next example is of an opposite sort. It comes from Volume IV, Part 3, Chapter 12: *Syódla i lózhki Zhiunó, oní ponimáli, shto moglí na shtó-nibud prigodítsya, no dlya chevó bylo golódnym i kholódnym soldátam stoyát na karaúle i steréch takíkh zhe kholódnykh i golódnykh rússkykh, kotórye myórli i ostaváli dorógoi, kotórykh véleno bylo pristrélivat – éto bylo ne tólko neponyátno, no i protívno.*
I remember reading somewhere that Tolstoy had made a special study of rhetoric and once boasted that in writing *War and Peace*

---

* The great Italian critic Francesco de Sanctis, in an essay comparing translations of *The Aeneid* by Annibale Caro and by Leopardi, characterizes the Roman poet's language as "this powerful Latin speech, which says so much in its imprecision" and chastises Caro for making it too explicit.

he had used every rhetorical device to be found in the old Latin grammarians. In the heterogeneous composition of the novel we find, along with the irreducible simplicity of *Kápli kápali,* a deliberately formal rhetoric, often far more elaborate than in the example just quoted, sometimes running for pages; though even my relatively brief example includes both periodic structure and chiasmus, a figure that is not uncommon in *War and Peace.* To capture the tonality of the original in a translation, it is necessary to keep both extremes of Tolstoy's style. Our version reads: "They understood that the saddles and Junot's spoons might be of some use, but why the hungry and cold soldiers had to stand guard and watch over equally cold and hungry Russians, who were dying and fell behind on the road, who were ordered to be shot – this was not only incomprehensible, but also repugnant." For some reason, perhaps simply inattention, none of my three English translators, nor even de Schloezer, keeps the chiasmus: *golódnym i kholódnym soldátam ... kholódnykh i golódnykh rússkykh.* Yet the figure could not be more deliberate. Does it matter? It did to Tolstoy, and I think it should to his translator.

This last is an example of what I would call Tolstoy's "signature style." He also had a fondness for larger rhetorical structures based on repeated triads of nouns, verbs, adjectives, and so on. In *Tolstoy: A Critical Introduction*, R. H. Christian, himself the translator of Tolstoy's diaries and letters, wrote:

> From the point of view of language and style, Tolstoy has been better served by his translators than many of his fellow countrymen. Nevertheless, standards fall a long way short of perfection. Clumsiness and *simplesse* apart, no English version of *War and Peace* has succeeded in conveying the power, balance, rhythm and above all the repetitiveness of the original. Perhaps it is repetition which is the most characteristic single feature of Tolstoy's prose style.

To illustrate his point he cites two passages, the second of which, in our translation, reads as follows:

> ... thought Prince Andrei, waiting among many significant and insignificant persons in Count Arakcheev's anteroom.

During his service, mostly as an adjutant, Prince
Andrei had seen many anterooms of significant per-
sons, and the differing characters of these anterooms
were very clear to him. Count Arakcheev's anteroom
had a completely special character. The insignificant
persons waiting in line for an audience in Count
Arakcheev's anteroom...

Christian notes that the Russian word *priémnaya* ("anteroom")
recurs five times in as many lines, and that the Maude transla-
tion glosses over that fact by omitting the word once and using
three different words for the rest. I will add that Mr. Briggs omits
the repeated word twice and varies it twice, while Constance
Garnett omits it only once, but otherwise keeps the repetitions,
coming closest to the original, as she so often does.

Let me end with a final paradox: Tolstoy, who scorned
writers of fine prose, calling them "hairdressers," who sought
"the shortest way to sense," who "wrote badly," made "school-
boy errors," whose literary ethic was founded on the imperative
to speak the truth – this Tolstoy was at the same time a highly
conscious artist, paid great attention to how he wrote, know-
ingly used "every rhetorical device in the old Latin grammar-
ians," could suggest the mentality of childhood by the structure
of a phrase, and could make silence itself audible in those four
brief sentences describing Petya's last night. My fellow New
Englander, the poet Robert Frost, was considered by many to
be a simple poet of country things. Once, after a public reading,
one of his simple country admirers raised the subject of all the
"tricks" used by modernist poets like Ezra Pound and T. S. Eliot,
and said: "You don't use any of these tricks, do you, Mr. Frost?"
Frost smiled wickedly and said: "I revel in them!" So did Tolstoy.
His translators owe their readers a share in that revelry.

COLOPHON

THE CAHIERS SERIES · NUMBER I
ISBN: 978-0-9552963-1-4

Printed by Principal Colour, Paddock
Wood, on Neptune Unique (text) and
Chagall (dust jacket). Set in Monotype
Dante by Giovanni Mardersteig.

Drawings: Alexander Pushkin
   (reproduced by permission of the
   Pushkinskii Dom, Moscow; courtesy
   of The School of Slavonic and East
   European Studies, London)
Series Editor: Dan Gunn
Design: Ornan Rotem

CENTER FOR WRITERS & TRANSLATORS
THE ARTS ARENA
THE AMERICAN UNIVERSITY OF PARIS

SYLPH EDITIONS, LEWES | 2007

THE ARTS ARENA

center for writers and translators

SYLPH
EDITIONS

www.aup.fr · www.sylpheditions.com

11 апрѣля
1821